THIS **Elephant & Piggie** BOOK
BELONGS TO:

Ariana and
Bobby

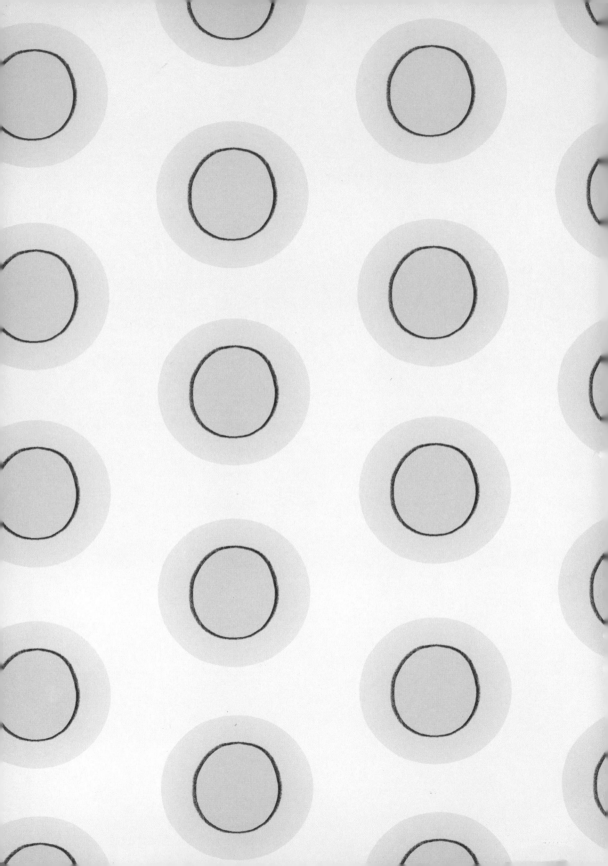

For Lowell, Lee
and Chelsea

Gerald!

Are you ready to play outside?

We are going
to skip!

PLINK!

It is starting to rain.

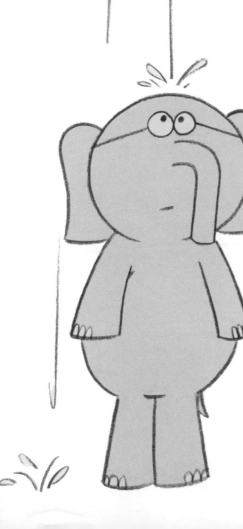

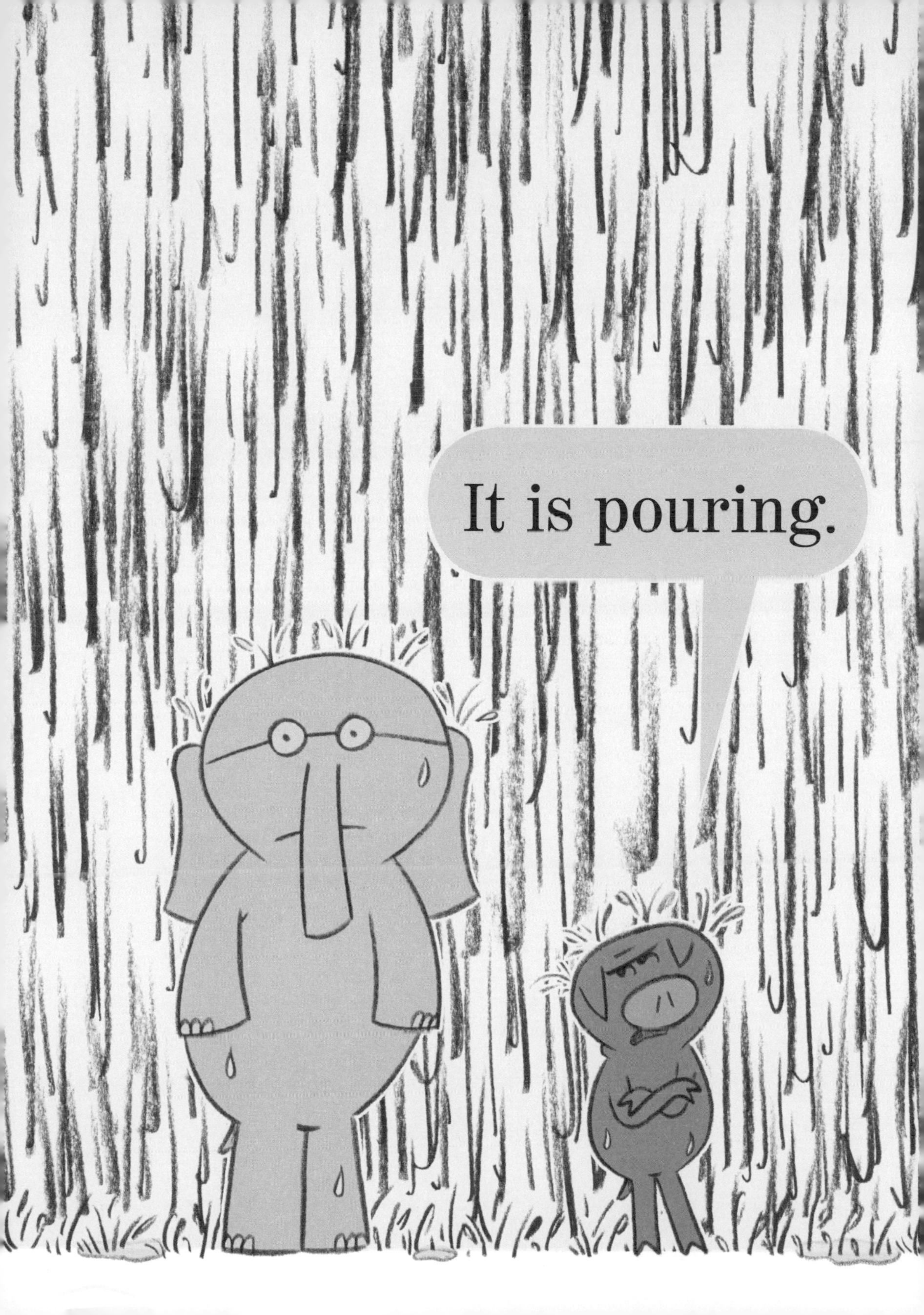
It is pouring.

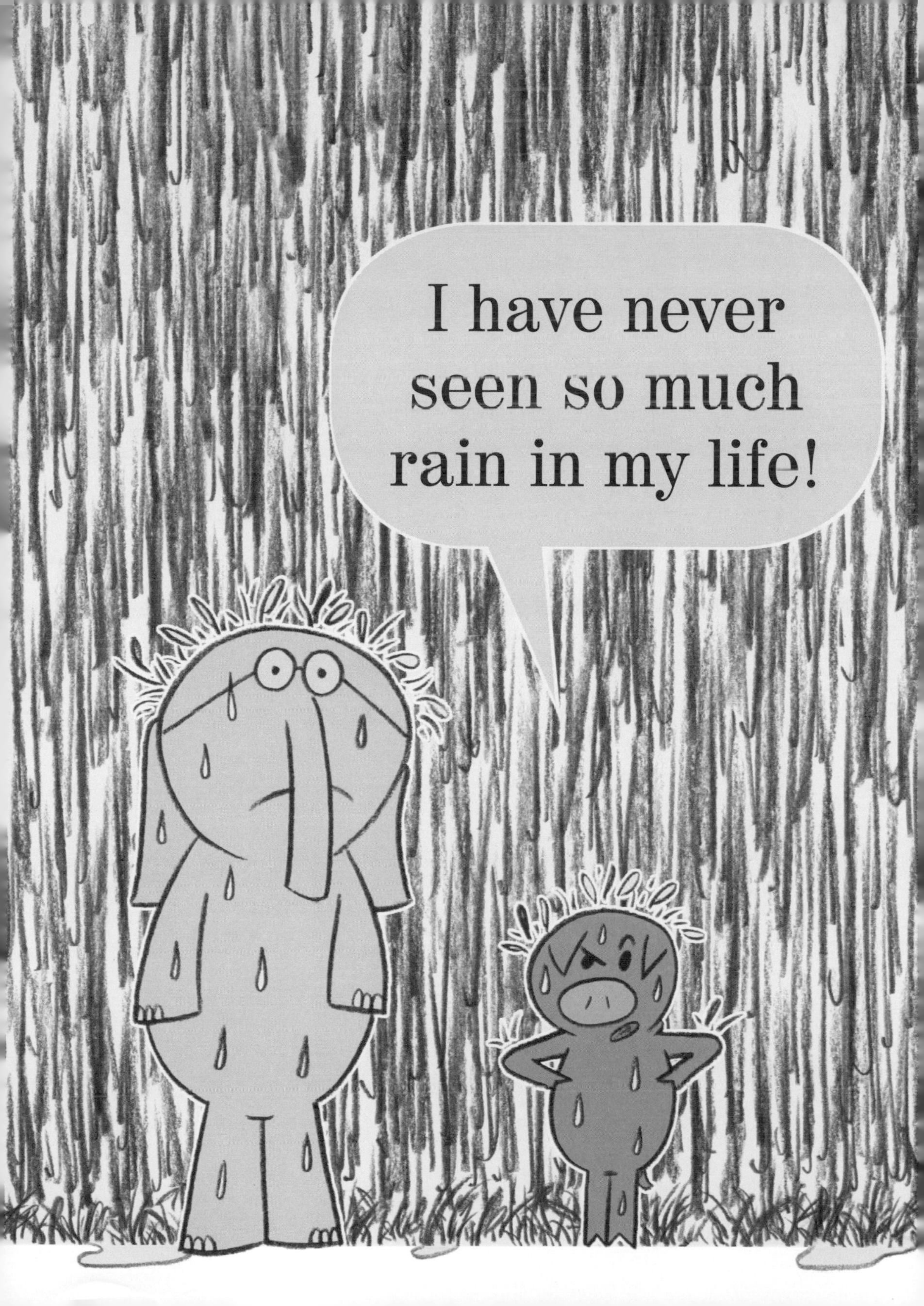
I have never seen so much rain in my life!

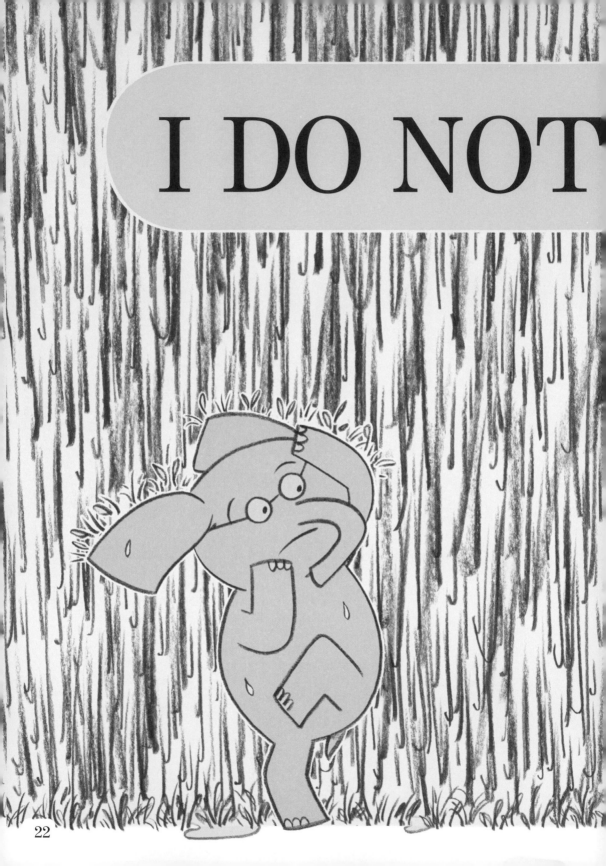

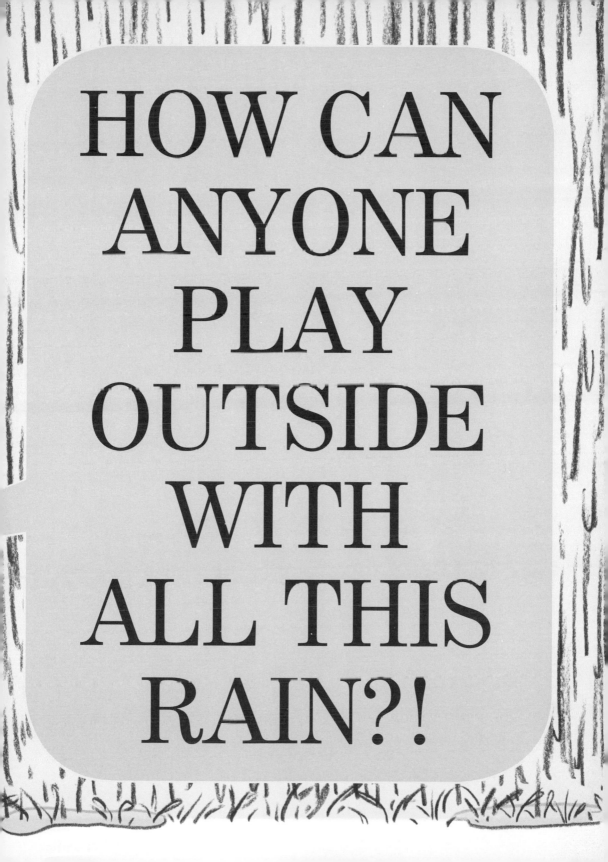

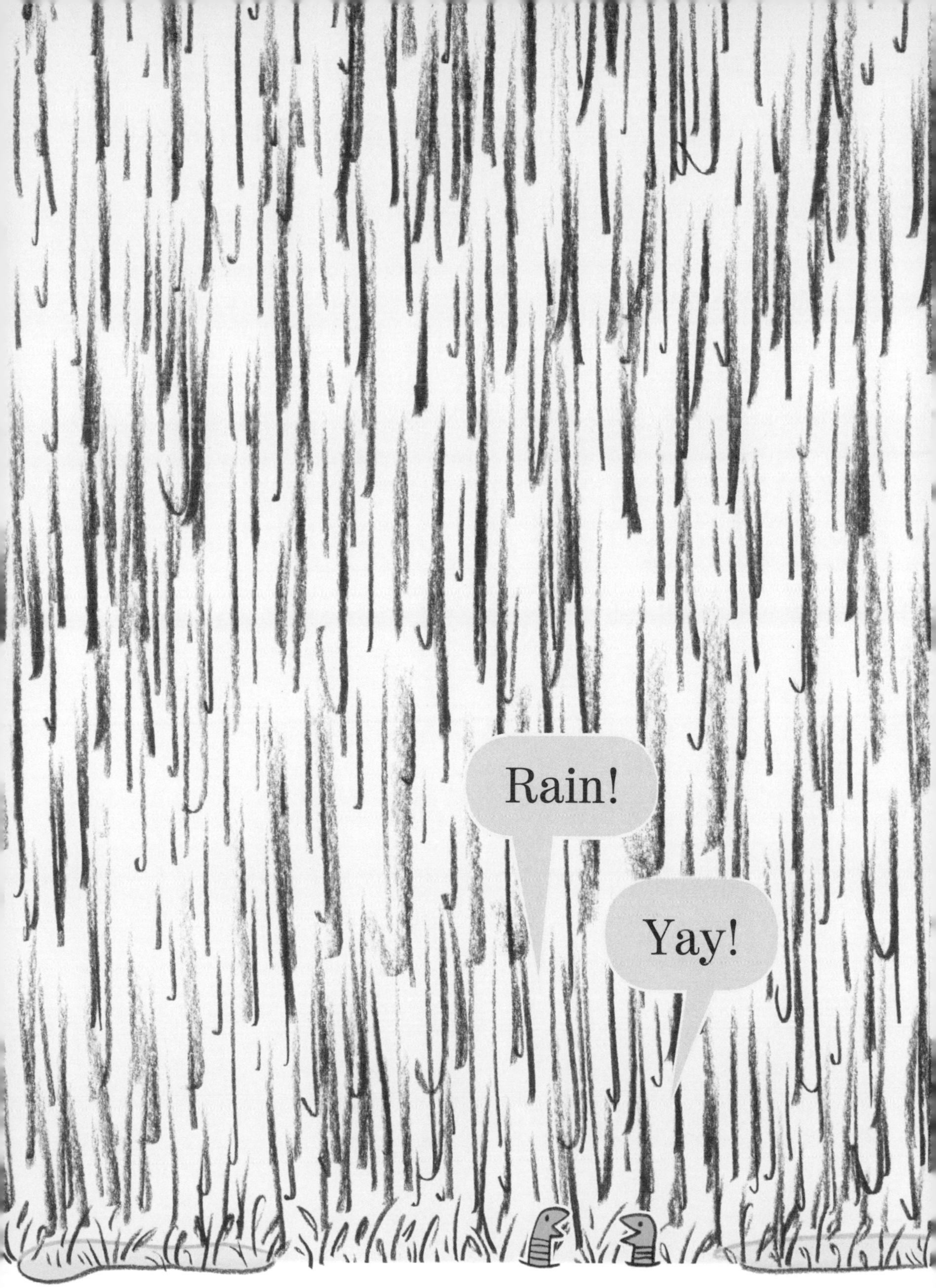
Rain!
Yay!

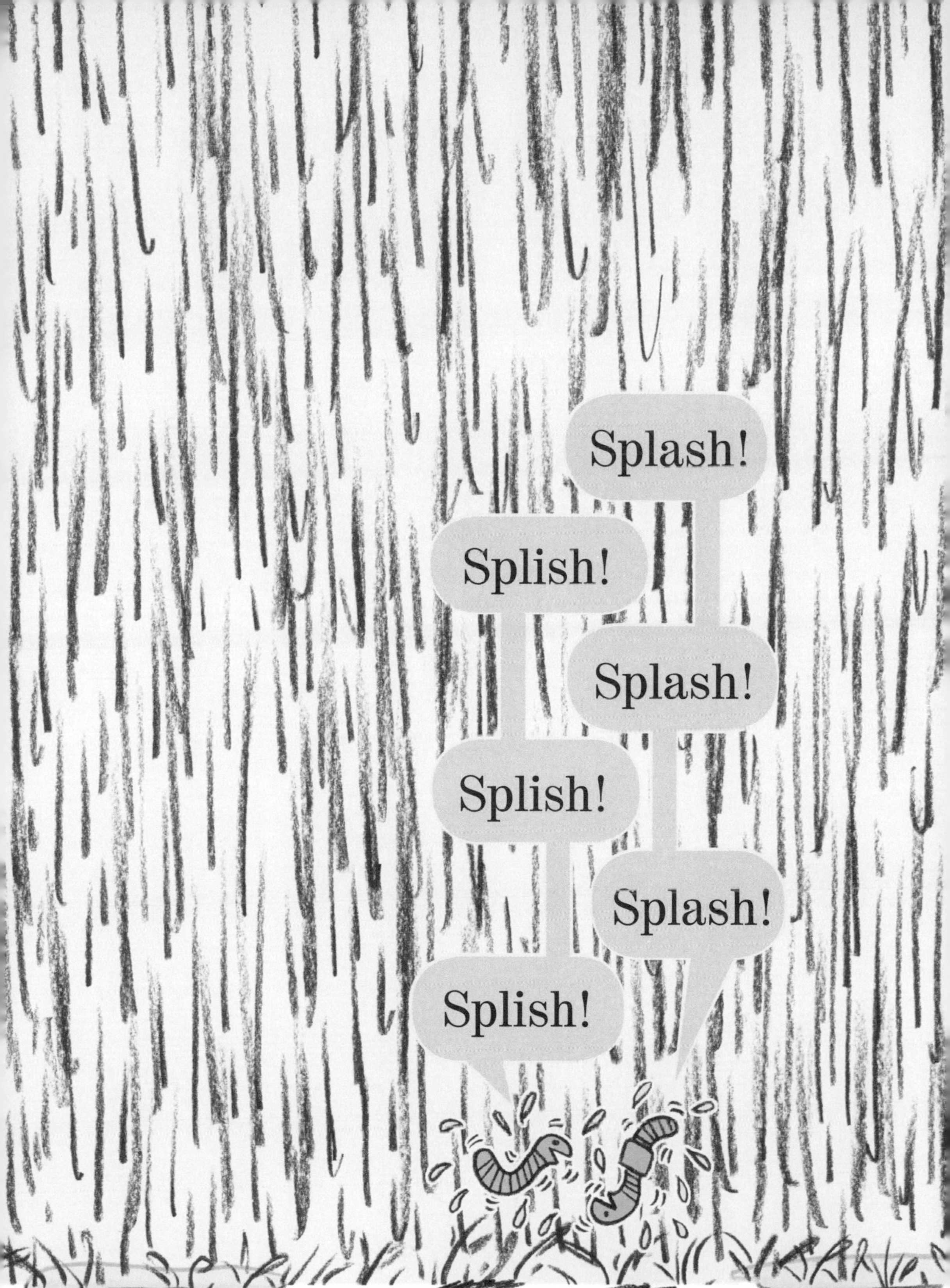
Splash!
Splish!
Splash!
Splish!
Splash!
Splish!

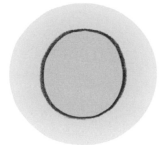

And now the rain has stopped!

I am not a happy pig.

56

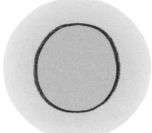

Do not worry, Piggie.
I have a plan.

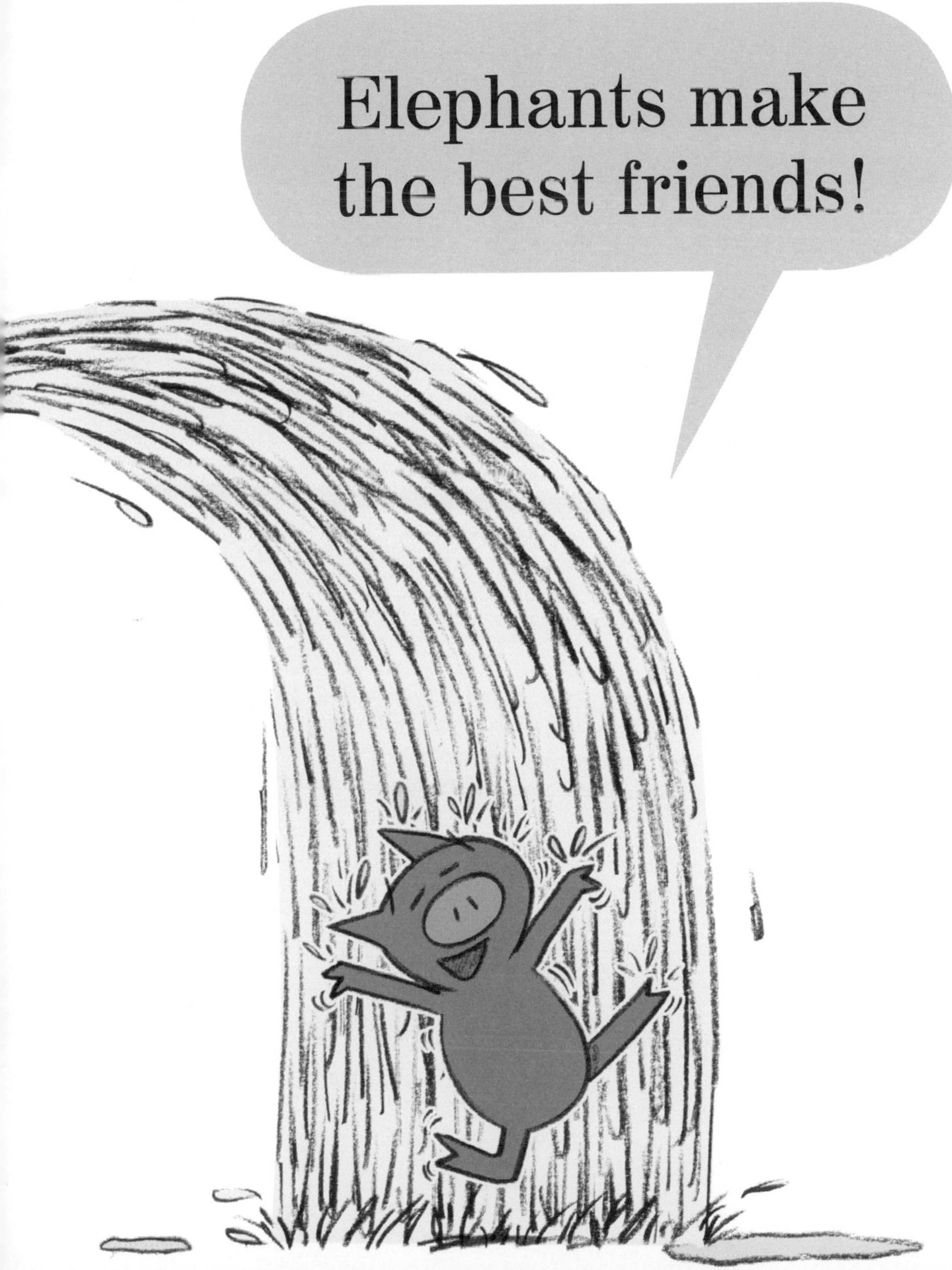
Elephants make the best friends!